WeeSing®
AROUND THE WORLD

by
Pamela Conn Beall and Susan Hagen Nipp
with Nancy Spence Klein

Illustrated by
Nancy Spence Klein

PRICE STERN SLOAN
Los Angeles

Special thanks to those who helped us with this book and tape:
United States (Omaha Indian)—Fletcher Conn, John Mangan, Elmer Blackbird; **Mexico**—Adriana Lazama Marquez, Mary Lindner; **Jamaica & Guyana**—Winston Cook; **Brazil**—Monica Rodrigues; **Argentina**—Mary Lindner, Argentina Lipowitz; **Peru**—Silvia Faust; **Norway**—Anna Mosey, Mia Shepard, Johanna Fedde; **Sweden**—Inga St. George, Ann Stuller; **Denmark**—Tanni Tytel; **Finland**—Pirjo Brooks, Rita Kazmierski, Sirpa Duoos; **Scotland**—Mary Pagach; **The Netherlands**—Lidwin Dirne; **Switzerland**—Elvira Tobler, Annemarie Harner, Shirley Abbott Clark; **Germany**—Renate Schlichting; **Spain**—Enrique Garciá, Manuela Thomas; **Italy**—Angela Barker, Riccardo Spaccarelli, Mirella Rizzatti; **Greece**—Theonie Gilmore, Betty Flevaris, Demetra Ariston, Gerasimos Tsirimiagos; **Ukraine**—Jania Yablonsky, Roy Torley; **Yugoslavia**—Aleksandra Markanovic; **Ghana**—Amowi Phillips, Esi Sutherland-Addy; **Nigeria**—Nnamdi Emetarom; **Zaire**—Zanga Malu; **Kenya**—Mary Mutitu; **Turkey**—Nilgun Emre, Emel Tunca; **Israel**—Elena Engel, Heidi Frankel, Joyce Shane; **Iran**—Malakeh Taleghani; **India**—Radhika Narayanan; **China**—Victor Chang, Mary Yeong, Janet Hagen, Eugenia Yau, Annette Chang; **Korea**—Kathy Jin Hagen, Reverend Jacob Chang Kim; **Japan**—Kumiko Jones, Ryuichi Yoshida; **Malaysia**—Norbaayah Mahari Young; **New Zealand**—Cynthia Fletcher; **Hawaii**—Janice Baisa, Gerald Markel. Also thanks to: Karen Ettinger, Theonie Gilmore, Kim Mogen, Janet Yoder, Whitworth College, Megan Wilson, Milan Robinson, Charlene Gebhardt, Jette Steuch, Vasiliki Ariston and Maya Narayanan.

A big thank you to our Wee Singers, Lindsay Beall, Emily Boucher, Kirsten Groener, Marika Groener, and to our music producer and arranger, Barry Hagen assisted by Mauri Macy and Dan Portis-Cathers.

Thanks also to our musicians who are listed on page sixty-four.

Our gratitude to Brian Healey for music engraving and typesetting.

Printed on recycled paper

Cover Illustration by Dennis Hockerman

Copyright © 1994 by Pamela Conn Beall and Susan Hagen Nipp
Published by Price Stern Sloan, Inc.
A member of The Putnam & Grosset Group, New York, New York.

ISBN: 0-8431-3740-1

10 9 8 7 6 5 4 3 2

PREFACE

What a wonderful and educational experience it has been to meet so many different people from around the world who were willing to share their music with us.

Music is truly a universal language and is an integral part of many societies. To hear and experience songs and music from different countries is to better understand the people who live there. Since our children today are becoming so much more aware of the world around them, we hope that *Wee Sing Around The World* will provide an experience that will make them want to learn more about children of different nationalities.

You'll enjoy hearing the many languages sung by people native to each country as well as the sounds of the authentic instruments. From a word–for–word translation we made our own poetic translation so children could better understand the song and be able to sing along in English as well as in the original language. We have stayed true to the overall meaning of the song even though each word is not always a literal translation. Provided also are some interesting facts about each country represented as well as instructions for actions, games and dances.

We are so thankful to all who have helped in the creation of this book and tape. They not only shared music; they shared their love for their country. We hope that all of you who experience listening, singing or reading along will gain a new appreciation for our diverse world. We certainly have!

Pam Beall
Susan Nipp

TABLE OF CONTENTS

Hello To All The Children Of The World 6
World Map 8

NORTH AMERICA

North America Map..9
Going Over The Sea *Canada* 10
Uhe′ Basho^n Sho^n (The Crooked Path) *United States* 12
Eentsy Weentsy Spider *United States* 13
Pin Pón *Mexico*...14
Tingalayo *West Indies*...15
El Coquí (The Frog) *Puerto Rico*..16
Chi Chi Bud (Chi Chi Bird) *Jamaica* 17

SOUTH AMERICA

South America Map...18
Brown Girl In The Ring *Guyana* 19
Ciranda (Circle Game) *Brazil*...20
Mi Chacra (My Farm) *Argentina*..22
Los Pollitos (The Little Chicks) *Peru* 24

EUROPE

Europe Map..25
Ro, Ro Til Fiskeskjær (Row, Row To The Fishing Spot) *Norway* ..26
Små Grodorna (Little Frogs) *Sweden* 27
En Enebær Busk (The Mulberry Bush) *Denmark* 28
Piiri Pieni Pyörii (The Circle Goes Around) *Finland* 30
Wee Falorie Man *Ireland*..31
Coulter's Candy *Scotland*...32
Lavender's Blue *England* 33
Alle Eendjes (All The Ducklings) *The Netherlands*.......................34
Frère Jacques (Brother John) *France* 35
Weggis Zue (Swiss Hiking Song) *Switzerland*...............................36
Alle Meine Entlein (All My Little Ducklings) *Germany*.................38
Mio Galletto (My Little Rooster) *Italy*...39
Mi Burro (My Burro) *Spain* 40
Pou 'n–do To Dachtilidi (Where Is The Ring) *Greece*.....................42
Ringe, Ringe Raja (Ring Around Raja) *Yugoslavia* 43
Vesyoliye Gusi (Jolly, Happy Ganders) *Ukraine* 44

AFRICA

Africa Map 45
Tue Tue *Ghana* 46
Akwa Nwa Nere Nnwa (The Little Nanny) *Nigeria* 47
Bebe Moke (Baby So Small) *Zaire* 48
Kanyoni Kanja (Little Bird Outside) *Kenya* 49

ASIA

Asia Map 50
Ali Babanin Çiftliği (Ali Baba's Farm) *Turkey* 51
Zum Gali Gali *Israel* 52
Attal, Mattal *Iran* 53
Anilae, Anilae (Chipmunk, Chipmunk) *India* 54
Kai Veechamma (Move Your Hand) *India* 54
Fong Swei (After School) *China* 55
Arirang *Korea* 56
Ame, Ame (Rain Song) *Japan* 57
Pok Amai, Amai (Clap Together) *Malaysia* 58

AUSTRALIA & OCEANIA

Australia & Oceania Map...59
Kookaburra *Australia*...60
Epo I Tai Tai E (I Will Be Happy) *New Zealand*.......................61
Nani Wale Na Hala (Pretty Hala Trees) *Hawaii*.......................62
Index 63

HELLO TO ALL THE CHILDREN OF THE WORLD

Nancy Klein
Nancy Klein
Pam Beall

Hel-lo, bon jour,* bue-nos di-as,* G'-day,* gu-ten Tag,* kon nich-i wa,* Ciao,* sha-lom,* do-brey dy-en,* Hel-lo to all the chil-dren of the world!

*These are greetings from the following countries:

bonjour—good day (French)
buenos dias—good day (Spanish)
g'day—good day (Australian)
guten Tag—good day (German)

kon nichi wa—hello (Japanese)
ciao—hi, good-bye (Italian)
shalom—hello, good-bye, peace (Hebrew)
dobrey dyen—good day (Russian)

India   Sweden   Nigeria   Korea

Verse

1. We live in diff'-rent pla-ces from all a-round the world, We speak in man-y diff'-rent ways__ Tho' some things might be diff'-rent, we're chil-dren just the same, And we all like to sing and play.

D.C. al Fine

2. There are children in the deserts
   And children in the towns
   And children who live down by the sea,
   If we could meet each other
   To run and sing and play,
   Then what good friends we all could be.
       Chorus

United States   Brazil   Germany   Hawaii

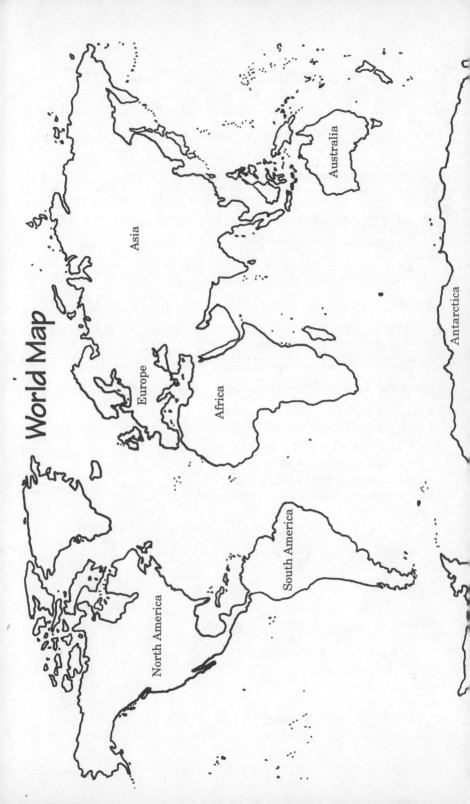

North America

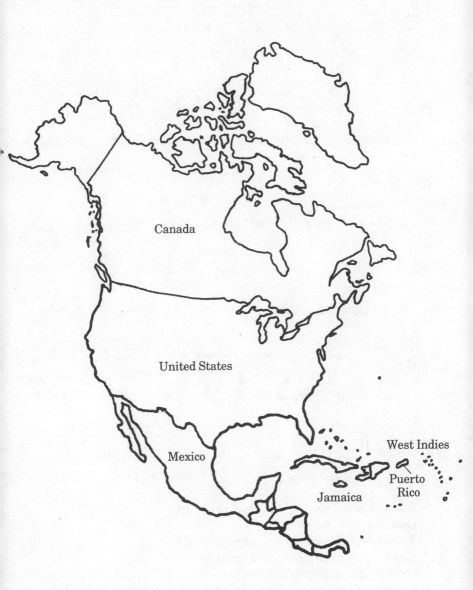

Canada

United States

Mexico

Jamaica

West Indies

Puerto
Rico

GOING OVER THE SEA

Canada

1. When I was ⓐone, I ate a bun, ⓑGo-ing o-ver the sea. I jumped a-board a sail-or-man's ship And the ⓓsail-or-man said to me, "Go-ing ⓔo-ver, go-ing ⓕun-der, Stand at at-ten-tion like a ⓗsol-dier With a ⓘone, two, three."

2. When I was ᵃtwo, I buckled my shoe,
   ᵇGoing over the sea.
   I ᶜjumped aboard a sailorman's ship
   And the ᵈsailorman said to me,
   "Going ᵉover, going ᶠunder,
   Stand at ᵍattention like a ʰsoldier
   With a ⁱone, two, three."

10

3. When I was [a]three, I banged my knee...
4. When I was [a]four, I shut the door...
5. When I was [a]five, I learned to dive...
6. When I was [a]six, I picked up sticks...
7. When I was [a]seven, I went to heaven...
8. When I was [a]eight, I learned to skate...
9. When I was [a]nine, I climbed a vine...
10. When I was [a]ten, I caught a hen...

Actions:
a) Hold up correct number of fingers
b) Shade eyes with hand
c) Jump once in place
d) Hands on hips
e) Swoop hand up
f) Swoop hand down
g) Stand erect with arms at sides
h) Salute with right hand
i) Step in place three times

Canada is the second largest country in the world but is not overly populated because of the harsh climate of the north. Most people live near the Canadian/U.S. border and many have either British or French ancestors. The two official languages of Canada are English and French. Indians and Inuits were the first inhabitants of Canada but now make up only 2% of the population.

11

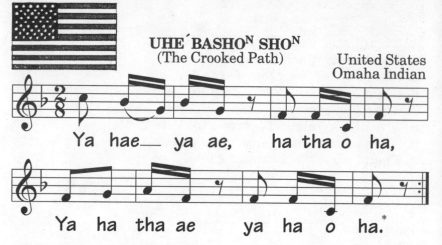

UHE´BASHO^N SHO^N
(The Crooked Path)

United States
Omaha Indian

Ya hae— ya ae, ha tha o ha,

Ya ha tha ae ya ha o ha.*

* These words have no particular meaning

Game: "Follow My Leader"

Formation: Children in line behind leader holding on to belt of person in front of him

Actions: Children follow the leader who starts off at a rapid jog-trot, keeping time to the song as all sing. Wherever the leader goes and whatever action he does, the children must follow (e.g. kick post, touch tree).

When Omaha Indian children played this game, they would "sing at the top of their voices and follow their leader wherever he went–through deserted earth lodges, the tall grass and mud puddles. Little beaded moccasins would be a sorry sight when they got through." (From *Oo-Mah-Ha Ta-Wa-Tha,* 1898, Omaha City, by Fannie Reed Giffen, Illustrated by Susette LaFlesche)

The Omaha Indians are a Midwestern Plains Indian tribe. They used to be great hunters of buffalo and wild game but turned to farming when the reservation was formed in Nebraska during the mid 1800's. They have always been a peaceful tribe and believe that education is the best way to compete in today's world.

EENTSY WEENTSY SPIDER

United States

@ The een-tsy, ween-tsy spi-der went up the wa-ter spout, ⓑ Down came the rain and ⓒ washed the spi-der out, ⓓ Out came the sun and ⓔ dried up all the rain, And the @ een-tsy, ween-tsy spi-der went up the spout a-gain.

Actions:
a) Make circles out of thumbs and forefingers, put tips together, twist upward
b) Wiggle fingers while moving downward
c) Push hands out to sides
d) Make big circle with arms over head
e) Hands in front, palms up, move up in rhythm

The first inhabitants of the United States were American Indians. European settlers began arriving in the 1500's. Today, the United States is a very diverse country because people from all over the world, representing different races, religions and nationalities, have settled in America. Through a spirit of cooperation and pride, they have built a very strong and rich nation.

PIN PÓN

1. Pin Pón es un mu-ñe-co de
   Pin Pon's a pa-per doll and his

tra-po y de car-tón, Se la-va su ca-
clothes are— all in place, He us-es soap and

ri-ta con a-gua y con ja-bón.
wa-ter to wash his— hands and face.

2. Se desenrreda el pelo
   Con peine de marfil,
   Y aunque se de estirones,
   No llora ni hace asi.

2. He straightens out his hair
   With a tiny ivory comb,
   And even if he pulls hard,
   He doesn't cry or moan.

Suggestion: Pantomime words to act out song.

Mexico was first inhabited by American Indians but was overtaken by Spaniards in the 1500's. It is now an independent country but Spanish is still the official language. The most important food in Mexico is corn and from cornmeal come tortillas which are used to make tacos and enchiladas. Children enjoy celebrations where piñatas are broken in a game. Piñatas are papier–mâché containers, often shaped like animals, filled with candy and toys.

14

TINGALAYO

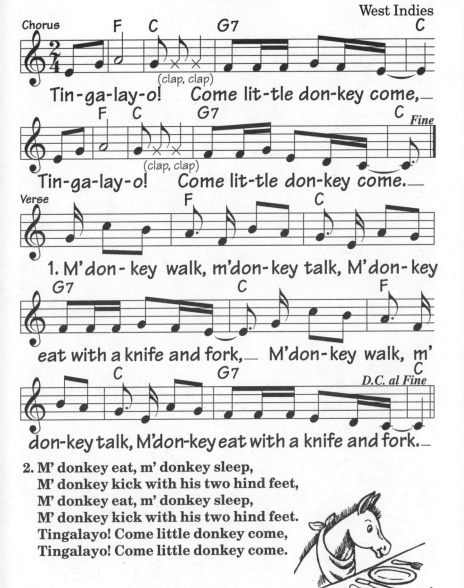

Chorus
F C   G7   C

Tin-ga-lay-o!   Come lit-tle don-key come,—
(clap, clap)

F C   G7   C *Fine*

Tin-ga-lay-o!   Come lit-tle don-key come.—
(clap, clap)

Verse
              F   C

1. M'don-key walk, m'don-key talk, M'don-key

G7   C   F

eat with a knife and fork,— M'don-key walk, m'

C   G7   C
                    D.C. al Fine

don-key talk, M'don-key eat with a knife and fork.—

2. M' donkey eat, m' donkey sleep,
   M' donkey kick with his two hind feet,
   M' donkey eat, m' donkey sleep,
   M' donkey kick with his two hind feet.
   Tingalayo! Come little donkey come,
   Tingalayo! Come little donkey come.

*The West Indies are a chain of tropical islands 2,000 miles long that separate the
Caribbean Sea from the rest of the Atlantic Ocean. The people who live there are mainly
of European or African ancestry. The steel drums, which are the only acoustic (non–elec-
tric) instruments invented in the twentieth century, originated on Trinidad, one of the
islands of the West Indies.*

15

EL COQUÍ
(The Frog)

Puerto Rico

El co-quí, el co-quí a mí me en-can-ta,
Lit-tle frog, lit-tle frog makes me hap-py,

Es tan lin-do el can-tar del co - quí,
With his sing-ing so love-ly and sweet,

Por las no - ches al ir a a-cos-tar-me,
When at night-time I lie down and lis - ten,

Me a-dor-me-ce can-tan - do a - sí.
It's his sing-ing that puts me to sleep.

Chorus

Co-quí, co-quí, co-quí, quí, quí, quí, Co-

quí, co - quí, co-quí, quí, quí, quí.

Puerto Rico is a U.S. commonwealth which means the people are American citizens but do not pay U.S. taxes or vote in presidential elections. Puerto Rico is the only part of the U.S. where Columbus is believed to have landed. Spanish is still the main language. Puerto Rico is famous for its sandy beaches and water sports.

CHI CHI BUD
(Chi Chi Bird)

Jamaica

Chorus

Chi chi bud, o! Some o' dem a hol - ler some a bawl! Chi chi bud, o! Some o' dem a hol - ler some a bawl!

Verse

Some a sea gull! Some o' dem a hol - ler some a bawl! Some a yel - low bird! Some o' dem a hol - ler some a bawl!

Suggestion: For more verses, repeat song as many times as desired, using names of different birds (e.g. parakeet, black bird, sparrow, bluebird, red bird).

Jamaica is an Indian word meaning "island of springs." This West Indies island used to be a British colony and the official language is English. Most of the people are of African ancestry. Because of Jamaica's beautiful beaches and mild climate, tourism has become an important industry.

South America

Guyana

Peru

Brazil

Argentina

BROWN GIRL IN THE RING

Guyana

1. There's a brown girl in the ring,— Tra-la-la-la-la, There's a brown girl in the ring,— Tra-la-la-la, There's a brown girl in the ring,— Tra-la-la-la-la,— She likes sug-ar and I like plum.

2. [b]Show me your motion, Tra-la-la-la-la,
   Show me your motion, Tra-la-la-la-la-la,
   Show me your motion, Tra-la-la-la-la,
   She likes sugar and I like plum.

3. [c]Skip across the ocean,...
   She likes sugar and I like plum.

4. [d]There's a brown boy in the ring,...
   He likes sugar and I like plum.

Formation:
Children in a circle, one girl in center

Actions:
a) Girl stands in center of circle as children sing and sway to the music
b) Girl does motion of her choosing, children sing and sway
c) Girl skips around inside circle, then chooses a boy
d) Boy stands in center of circle and game begins again

Guyana is a tropical country with large sugar plantations. It was a British colony until 1966 and the official language is English. Most people are East Indian or African whose ancestors were brought to work on the sugar plantations.

CIRANDA
(Circle Game)

Brazil

1. Ci-ran-da, ci-ran-di-nha, Va-mos
Ci-ran-da, ci-ran-di-nha, Let's all

to-dos ci-ran-dar, Va-mos dar a
join our hands and play, Skip half way a-

me-ia vol-ta, Vol-ta e me-ia va-mos dar.
round the cir-cle, Turn and go the oth-er way.

2. ^cO anel que tu me deste
Era vidro e se quebrou,
O amor que tu me tinhas
Era pouco e se acabou.

3. ^cPor isto Dona Gina (Senhor Marcelo)
Entre dentro desta roda;
Diga um verso bem bonito,
Diga adeus e vase embora.^d

Poem
Sou peque' nininha,
Do tamanho de um botāo,
Carrego papai no bolço e
Mamāe no coração.

2. [c]The little ring you gave me,
   It was only made of glass,
   And the love you said you had for me
   Was small and didn't last.
3. [c]And so we call Miss Gina (Sir Marcelo),
   Step inside our circle please,
   Say a verse all by yourself
   Then say good-bye and you may leave.[d]

Poem

I'm little like a button
  (thumb and pointer finger make circle)
And when we are apart,
  (hold hands apart)
I bring Daddy in my pocket
  (pretend to put something in pocket over heart)
And Mommy in my heart.
  (cross hands over heart)

Formation: Children in circle holding hands. One by one they will be called to the center of the circle.

Actions:
a) Circle left, skipping
b) Quickly reverse direction and circle right, skipping
c) Continue circling right
d) Stop circling. Named child enters circle and says a poem of choice such as a nursery rhyme. Child returns to circle and game begins again.

Brazil is the largest country in South America and the only one whose official language is Portuguese. The world's largest tropical rain forest is in Brazil and the Amazon River flows through it. Festivals are famous in Brazil, the best known being Carnival with exciting parades and colorful dancers.

21

MI CHACRA
(My Farm)
Argentina

1. Ven - gan a ver mi cha - cra que es her-
Come see my lit - tle farm for it is

mo - sa, Ven - gan a ver mi
beau - ti - ful, Come see my lit - tle

cha - cra que es her - mo - sa,
farm for it is beau - ti - ful,

El po - lli - to ha - ce a - sí, "pio, pio,"
Lit - tle chick-en goes like this, "peep, peep,"

El po - lli - to ha - ce a - sí, "pio, pio,"
Lit - tle chick-en goes like this, "peep, peep,"

Chorus

O vas, cam - a - rad - a, vas, cam - a-
Oh, come now my friend, oh, come now my

rad - a, vas, o vas, o vas, O
friend, Oh come, oh come, oh come, Oh,

vas, cam - a - rad - a, vas, cam - a -
come now my friend, oh, come now my

rad - a, vas, o vas, o vas.
friend, Oh come, oh come, oh come.

2. Vengan a ver mi chacra que es hermosa,
   Vengan a ver mi chacra que es hermosa,
   El patito hace así, "cua, cua,"
   El patito hace así, "cua, cua,"
       Chorus
3. ...el chanchito... "oinc, oinc"...
4. ...el gatito... "mi-au"...
5. ...el perrito... "guau, guau"...
6. ...el burrito... "ji-jo"...

2. Come see my little farm for it is beautiful,
   Come see my little farm for it is beautiful,
   Little duckling goes like this, "quack, quack,"
   Little duckling goes like this, "quack, quack,"
       Chorus
3. ...little piglet... "oink, oink"...
4. ...little kitten... "meow, meow"...
5. ...little puppy... "bow wow"...
6. ...little donkey... "hee-haw"...

Argentina is a wealthy country whose people are mostly of Spanish and Italian descent. There are many large cattle ranches in Argentina making it one of the world's leaders in production of beef and hides. Many legends, songs, and paintings were inspired by gauchos (Argentine cowboys).

23

LOS POLLITOS
(The Little Chicks)

Peru

1. Los po-lli-tos di - cen, "pí - o,
All the lit - tle chicks say, "peep, peep,

pí - o, pí - o," Cuan - do tien-en
peep, peep, peep,"— When they're feel-ing

ham - bre cuan - do tien - en frí - o.
cold and need some food to eat.—

2. La gallina busca el maíz el trigo,
Y les dá comida y les presta abrigo.

3. Los pollitos duermen acurracaditos
Bajo de sus alas hasta el otro diá.
Pío, pío, pío, pío, pío, pá.
Pío, pío, pío, pío, pío, pá.

2. Mother hen goes looking for some corn and wheat,
Then she feeds the chicks and cuddles them to sleep.

3. Underneath her warm wings, all night long they sleep,
'Til the sun awakes them and they start to peep.
Pío, pío, pío, pío, pío, pá.
Pío, pío, pío, pío, pío, pá.

Suggestion: Pantomime words to act out song.

Peru has great extremes in landscape and climate, from the snowcapped Andes Mountains to thick rain forests (jungles). Most Peruvians are Indians or mestizos (Indian and Spanish) and their ancestors include the great Inca Indians who had a vast, rich empire from the 1200's to the 1500's.

24

Europe

Scotland

Ireland

Denmark

The
Nether-
lands

England

Norway

Sweden

Finland

Russia

Germany

France

Switzerland

Ukraine

Spain

Italy

Former
Yugoslovia

Greece

RO, RO TIL FISKESKJÆR
(Row, Row To The Fishing Spot)
Norway

Ro, ro til fis - ke - skjær, hvor
Row, row to the fish - ing spot, how

man - ge fis - ker får vi der? En til
man - y big fish will be caught? One for

far og en til mor,— en til søs - ter,
fath - er, one for moth - er, one for sis - ter,

en til bror, Og en til den som fis - ken
one for broth - er, One is for the fish - er -

fann, og det var ves - le O - lav mann.
man and that is lit - tle O - lav man.

Formation: Partners sit on floor facing each other, feet touching, holding hands.

Actions: Rock back and forth as if rowing a boat.

Norway is known for its beautiful fjords (long, narrow inlets of the sea) that jut into the rocky coastline. The northern third of Norway lies above the Arctic Circle and is called the "Land of the Midnight Sun" because the sun never sets during part of the summer.

SMÅ GRODORNA
(Little Frogs)

Sweden

1. Små gro-dor-na, små gro-dor - na är
The lit-tle frogs, the lit - tle frogs are

G7

lus-ti-ga att se, Små gro-dor-na, små
lots of fun to watch, The lit - tle frogs, the

C

gro-dor - na är lus-ti-ga att se.
lit - tle frogs are lots of fun to watch.

2. [b]Ej öron, ej öron, [c]ej svansar hava de,
  [b]Ej öron, ej öron, [c]ej svansar hava de.

3. [d]Kou-ack-ack-ack, kou-ack-ack-ack,
  kou-ack-ack-ack-ack-ack-a,
  [d]Kou-ack-ack-ack, kou-ack-ack-ack,
  kou-ack-ack-ack-ack-ack-a.

2. [b]No ears, no ears, [c]no tails have they,
  [b]No ears, no ears, [c]no tails have they.

3. [d]Kou-ack-ack-ack...

Formation: Children in circle, holding hands

Actions:
a) Circle left
b) Continue to circle, release hands, flap hands by ears
c) Flap hands behind back while circling
d) Hands on hips, hop around circle

Sweden is one of the most prosperous countries in the world. There are no slums in the cities and few people are very poor. Sweden, Norway, and Denmark are called Scandinavia. They share similar languages and cultures. Swedish children love to sing this song around the maypole in June during Midsummer festival and at Christmas time around the Christmas tree.

EN ENEBÆR BUSK
(The Mulberry Bush)

Denmark

1. Så går vi rundt om en e - ne - bær busk,
We dance a-round the—mul-ber-ry bush,

E - ne - bær busk, e - ne - bær busk,
Mul-ber-ry bush, mul-ber-ry bush,

Så går vi rundt om en e - ne - bær busk,
We dance a-round the— mul-ber-ry bush,

Tid - lig en man - dag mor - gen.
Ear - ly— Mon - day morn - ing.

2. ᵇSå gør vi sådan når vi vasker vort tøj,
   Vasker vort tøj, vasker vort tøj,
   Så gør vi sådan når vi vasker vort tøj,
   Tidlig en tirsdag morgen.
3. ᶜ...vrider vort tøj...onsdag
4. ᶜ...hænger vort tøj...torsdag
5. ᶜ...stryger vort tøj...fredag
6. ᶜ...folder vort tøj...lørdag
7. ᵈ...(til) kirke vi går...søndag

28

2. [b]We do this when we wash our clothes,
   Wash our clothes, wash our clothes,
   We do this when we wash our clothes
   Early Tuesday morning.

3. [c]...wring our clothes...Wednesday

4. [c]...hang our clothes...Thursday

5. [c]...iron our clothes...Friday

6. [c]...fold our clothes...Saturday

7. [d]...go to church...Sunday

Formation:
Children in circle, holding hands.

Actions:
a) Circle left
b) Pantomime washing clothes on washboard
c) Pantomime words
d) Walk arm in arm

Denmark is a country almost entirely surrounded by water. It consists of a mainland peninsula (land projecting out into water) plus 482 islands. At least half the people use bicycles for transportation. Danes are famous for their buttery Danish pastry. One of Denmark's most famous writers was Hans Christian Andersen who wrote many fairy tales.

29

PIIRI PIENI PYÖRII
(The Circle Goes Around)
Finland

1. Pii - ri pie - ni pyö- rii, Lap- set
'Round and 'round the cir- cle, Chil-dren

sii - nä hyö- rii, Sor- met sa - noo
'round the cir- cle, Fin - gers point- ing

so, so, so, Ken - gän kan-nat ko, ko, ko.
so, so, so, Shoes are tap-ping ko, ko, ko.

2. ªPiiri pieni pyörii,
   Lapset siinä hyörii,
   ᶠKädet panee ᵍlip, lap, lap,
   ᵈKengän kannat ʰkip, kap, kap.

2. ª'Round and 'round the circle,
   Children 'round the circle,
   ᶠHands are saying ᵍlip, lap, lap,
   ᵈHeels are clicking ʰkip, kap, kap.

Formation:
Children in circle, holding hands

Actions:
a) Circle around
b) Stop circling, point index fingers
c) Do "scolding" motion three times
d) Point to feet
e) Stamp feet three times
f) Stop circling, hold up hands
g) Clap hands three times
h) Click heels together three times

Finland has thousands of lakes and more than two thirds of the land is covered with thick forests . In winter,the lakes freeze and the people enjoy ice hockey and ice skating. Saunas have been a tradition in Finland for 1,000 years. Bathers sit in a very small heated room or bath house, then swim or take a cold shower.

WEE FALORIE MAN

Ireland

1. I am the wee fa-lo-rie† man, A
rat-tlin' ro-vin' I-rish-man,
I can do all that ev-er you can, For
I am the wee fa-lo-rie man.___

2. I am a good old workin' man,
   Each day I carry my wee tin can,
   A large penny bap* and a clipe** of ham,
   I am a good old workin' man.

† unique, interesting fellow
* small loaf of bread
** large hunk

Ireland is called the "Emerald Isle" because of its green countryside of rolling hills and farmland. St. Patrick, the patron saint of Ireland, introduced Christianity to Ireland in the 400's. St. Patrick's Day is widely celebrated in his honor. Famous in Irish folklore is the leprechaun, a little man who reveals hidden treasures to anyone who catches him.

COULTER'S CANDY

Scotland

Chorus

Al - ly bal - ly, al - ly bal - ly bee, Sit - tin'
on your mam - my's knee, Greet - in' fur an-
ith-er* baw-bee* Tae* buy mair* Coul-ter's can - dy.

Verse (same tune as chorus)

1. Mammy, gie* me ma* thrifty* doon,*
   Here's auld* Coulter comin' roon,*
   Wi' a basket on his croon,*
   Sellin' Coulter's candy.

   Chorus

2. Little Annie's greetin', tae,*
   Sae* whit* can her puir* Mammy dae,*
   But gie them a penny a'tween them twae*
   Tae buy mair Coulter's candy.

   Chorus

*meaning listed below:

greetin'–cryin'	auld–old
anither–another	roon–round
bawbee–coin	croon–head
tae–to, too	sae–so
mair–more	whit–what
gie–give	puir–poor
ma–my	dae–do
thrifty–bank	twae–two
doon–down	

Scotland is part of Great Britain, along with England, Northern Ireland and Wales. In the 1800's, Mr. Coulter peddled candy in the streets of Kelso, Scotland, with a basket on his head. In Scotland, the bagpipe is the national instrument. Many Scots still wear kilts (a type of pleated skirt made from a plaid cloth).

LAVENDER'S BLUE*

England

1. Lav-en-der's blue, did-dle, did-dle,
Lav-en-der's green; When I am
King, did-dle, did-dle, You shall be Queen.

2. Call to your men, diddle, diddle,
   Set them to work;
   Some to the plough, diddle, diddle,
   Some to the cart.

3. Some to make hay, diddle, diddle,
   Some to cut corn;
   While you and I, diddle, diddle,
   Keep ourselves warm.

* Lavender is a plant of the mint family with fragrant bluish–purple flowers.

For hundreds of years, England was one of the world's most powerful countries. It is known for its long tradition of kings and queens, but now the country is actually ruled by a prime minister and Parliament.

ALLE EENDJES
(All The Ducklings)
The Netherlands

1. Al - le eend - jes zwem - men in het wa - ter,
All the duck - lings swim - ming in the wa - ter,

Fal - de - ral - de - rie - re, fal - de - ral - de - rie - re,

Al - le eend - jes zwem - men in het wa - ter,
All the duck - lings swim - ming in the wa - ter,

Fal - de - ral - de, ral - de - ral - de - ra.

2. Alle vissen zwemmen in het water,
   Fal-de-ral-de-rie-re, fal-de-ral-de-rie-re,
   Alle vissen zwemmen in het water,
   Fal-de-ral-de, ral-de-ral-de-ra.
3. Alle kinderen...

2. All the fishes swimming in the water...
3. All the children...

The Netherlands is often called "Holland" and the people are referred to as "Dutch." They used to be known for wearing wooden shoes (klompen) and are still famous for growing tulips. Much of The Netherlands is below sea level so water is continuously pumped into canals (now by electricity, originally by windmills).

34

FRÈRE JACQUES
(Brother John)
(Round)

France

1. Frè-re Jac-ques, Frè-re Jac-ques,
Are you sleep-ing, Are you sleep-ing,

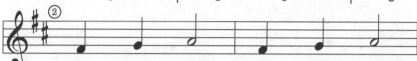

Dor-mez vous, Dor-mez vous?
Broth-er John, Broth-er John?

Son-nez les ma-ti-nes, Son-nez les ma-
Morn-ing bells are ring-ing, Morn-ing bells are

ti-nes, Ding, dang, dong! Ding, dang, dong!
ring-ing, Ding, dang, dong! Ding, dang, dong!

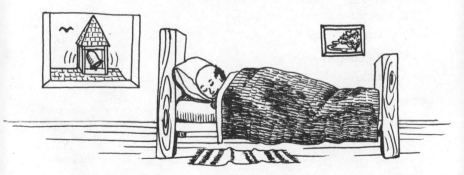

France is known for its great artists, including Monet, Renoir and Rodin. The Louvre, one of the world's largest art museums, is in Paris, the country's capital. The French are famous for their cooking, which is also considered an art. The Statue of Liberty was a gift from France to the United States in 1884.

WEGGIS ZUE
(Swiss Hiking Song)

Switzerland
Johann Luthi
(1800–1869)

Adapted

1. Vo Lu-zern ge-ge Weg-gis zue,
From Lu-cern walk to Weg-gis fine,

Yo lo lo oo ree ree o lo lo lo oo roo,

Brucht mer währ-li___ Strumpf nur Schueh,
Shoes and socks we can leave be-hind,

Yo lo lo oo ree ree o lo.

Chorus

Oo hoo doo doo doo dee dee dee o,

Yo lo lo oo ree ree o lo lo lo oo roo

Oo hoo doo doo doo dee dee dee o,

Yo lo lo oo ree ree o lo.

2. **Mer cha fahre übere See,**
   Yo lo lo oo ree ree o lo lo oo roo,
   Und cha schöni Fischli gseh,
   Yo lo lo oo ree ree o lo.
        Chorus

2. Come, go out on the lake with me,
   Yo lo lo oo ree ree o lo lo lo oo roo,
   We will find pretty fish to see,
   Yo lo lo oo ree ree o lo.
        Chorus

Switzerland is a small country with many mountains. The Swiss people used to yodel with their voices in the mountains and enjoy the echoes. They found that the sound carried well and it was a good way to communicate with others. There are three official languages in Switzerland—German, French and Italian.

ALLE MEINE ENTLEIN
(All My Little Ducklings)

Germany

Al - le mei - ne Ent - lein Schwim - men
All my lit - tle duck-lings swim - ming

ü - ber'n See; s'Kop - ferl in dem
here and there; Heads are in the

Was - ser, Schwänz - chen in der Höh.
wa - ter, tails are in the air.

*Germany is a country dotted with many old castles built in the Middle Ages. East
Germany and West Germany, divided since World War II, became one country again in
1990. Many great musicians were German including Bach, Handel and Brahms.
Hamburgers and hot dogs (frankfurters) originated in Germany and were named after
the towns of Hamburg and Frankfurt.*

MIO GALLETTO
(My Little Rooster)

Italy

L'o per-dut-to il mi - o gal - let - to,
Oh, I lost my— sweet lit-tle roos-ter,

L'o per-dut-to e l'o tro - vat - to,
Oh, I lost him,— then I found him,

L'o tro - vat - to po - ver - et - to,
Oh, I found my dear, sweet roos-ter,

Che fa - ce - va chi chi - ri chi.
When he chant-ed ki ki - ri ki.

Italy is known for its beautiful architecture, famous artists and ancient ruins. Opera was developed in Italy. The Pope, spiritual leader of the Roman Catholic Church, lives in Vatican City in Rome. Pizza, now a popular food around the world, originated in Italy.

MI BURRO
(My Burro)

Spain

1. A mi bur - ro,* mi bur - ro, le
Oh, my bur - ro, my bur - ro, his

duel - e le ca - be - za, Y el med - i -
head is ach - ing bad - ly, The doc - tor

co le ha da - do un - a gor - ri - ta
gave my bur - ro a stock - ing cap to

grue - sa. Un - a gor - ri - ta
wear.___ A stock - ing cap, a

grue - sa, Mi bur - ro en - fer - mo e -
stocking cap, My bur - ro is not

sta, mi bur - ro en - fer - mo e - sta.
well, my bur - ro is not well.

2. A mi burro, mi burro, le duele la garganta,
   Y el medico le ha dado una bufanda blanca.
   Una bufanda blanca, una gorrita gruesa,
   Mi burro enfermo esta, mi burro enfermo esta.
3. A mi burro, mi burro, le duele el corazon,
   Y el medico le ha dado gotitas de limon.
   Gotitas de limon, una bufanda blanca, una gorrita gruesa,
   Mi burro enfermo esta, mi burro enfermo esta.

2. Oh, my burro, my burro, his throat is aching badly,
   The doctor gave my burro a long white scarf to wear.
   A white scarf, a stocking cap,
   My burro is not well, my burro is not well.
3. Oh, my burro, my burro, his heart is aching badly,
   The doctor gave my burro some drops of lemon juice.
   Some lemon juice, a white scarf, a stocking cap,
   My burro is not well, my burro is not well.

* a small donkey used as a pack animal because it is sure-footed

Spain at one time had many explorers who claimed much of the Americas. Spanish is still spoken in many of these countries. Today Spain is known for sunny weather, beautiful beaches, bullfights, and colorful dances. The famous artist Pablo Picasso was from Spain.

POU 'N–DO TO DACHTILIDI
(Where Is The Ring)

Greece

Pou 'n-do, pou 'n-do to dach-ti-li-di,
Where, oh where, oh where is the ring, Oh,

Psa - kse, psa-kse den tha to vris?
where's the ring, the ring that we hide?

Den tha to vris, den tha to vris
You will not find, you will not find,

To dach-ti-li-di o-pou zi-tis.
You will not find the ring, but please try.

Formation: All stand in circle, hands in front, palms together with fingers pointing to center of circle. Slightly cup hands. "Leader" is in center of circle with a ring hidden in his cupped hands.

Actions: Leader goes around circle pretending to drop hidden ring into children's hands. Secretly the ring is dropped into the cupped hands of one of the children but leader continues pretending until end of song. "It" is chosen by the leader to guess who has the ring. If "it" guesses correctly, he becomes the new leader. If "it" does not choose correctly, the leader remains the same and the child with the ring becomes the new "it."

Που 'ναι το, Που 'ναι το
τό δαχτυλίδι,
ψάζε, ψάζε δέν θά τό
βρεῖς,
Δέν θά τό βρεῖς, δέν θά
τό βρεῖς,
Τό δαχτυλίδι ὅπον ζητεῖς.

Lyrics in Greek

The achievements of the ancient Greeks in government, science, philosophy, the arts and sports still influence our lives today. Historic ruins from structures over 2,000 years old still stand. The original Olympic games began in Greece, probably before 1400 B.C.

42

RINGE, RINGE RAJA
(Ring Around Raja)
Yugoslavia

Rin - ge, rin - ge, Ra - ja, Do - šo Či - ka
Ring - a, ring - a, Ra - ja, Here comes Grand - pa

Pa - ja, Pa po - je - o ja - ja, je - dno ja - je
Pa - ja, He ate all the eggs and one egg sound - ed

"muć!" A mi dje - co ćuć.
"mooch!" Chil - dren all fall down.

Formation: Children in circle, holding hands.

Actions: Circle around holding hands. On the last word, squat or fall down.

*This is the flag of Yugoslavia before 1991.

Yugoslavia was a diverse country with many different cultures and customs. It broke into several independent nations in 1991. The traditions of these cultures have been preserved through music, dance, stories, and costumes. This game song is known in many areas of the former Yugoslavia.

43

VESYOLIYE GUSI
(Jolly, Happy Ganders)

Ukraine

Ji - li u ba - bu - si, Dva ve -
Gran-ny has two gan-ders, Jol - ly,

syo - lich gu - sya, O - din sa - ree,
hap - py gan-ders, One is gray and

dru - goi be - llee Dva ve-syo-lich gu - sya.
one is white, Those jol-ly, hap-py gan-ders.

2. **Mili gusi lapki**
   Okolo kanafki,
   Odin saree, drugoi bellee
   Okolo kanafki.
   Odin saree, drugoi bellee
   Okolo kanafki.

Жили у бабуси
два веселых гуся
Один серый,
другой белый,
Два веселых гуся (2 раза)

2. See them splash and waddle,
   Washing in the puddle,
   One is gray and one is white,
   They're washing in the puddle.
   One is gray and one is white,
   They're washing in the puddle.

Lyrics in Russian

The Ukraine is a country of rich farmlands, mining and industry. Until 1991, the Ukraine was a part of the Soviet Union (sometimes called Russia). This song is in Russian, but the official language of the Ukraine is now Ukrainian.

Africa

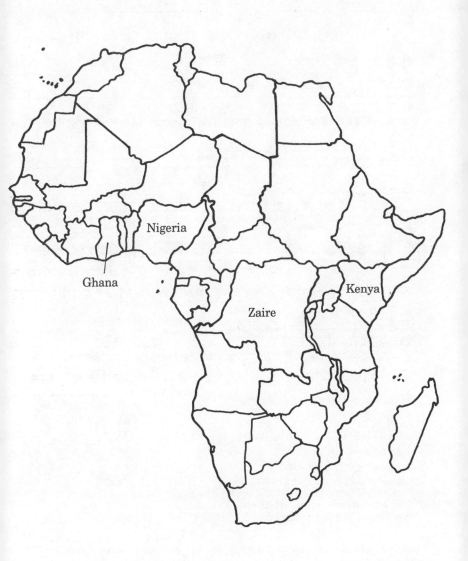

Nigeria

Ghana

Zaire

Kenya

TUE TUE *

Ghana

ⓐTu-e tu-e ⓑba-ri-ma ©tu-e tu-e ⓓ

ⓐTu-e tu-e ⓑba-ri-ma ©tu-e tu-e ⓓ A-bo-fra

ⓐba a-ma ⓑda-wa da-wa ©tu-e tu-e ⓓ A-bo-fra

ⓐba a-ma ⓑda-wa da-wa ⓐtu-e tu-e

ⓓHei! Ba-ri-ma ⓐtu-e tu-e ⓑHei! Ba-ri-ma

Formation:
Children stand in a circle. Turn to face a partner.

Actions:
a) Tap own thighs twice
b) Tap partner's hands twice in air
c) Turn to face partner on other side and tap own thighs twice
d) Tap new partner's hands twice in air.
   Repeat the last line several times getting faster, louder, and more vigorous, ending on "Hei!"

*The words of this song come from a combination of languages and have no particular meaning.

There are many different languages spoken in Ghana but English is the official language. Ghana is the world's leading exporter of cacao which is used to make chocolate. Also from Ghana comes kente, a famous colorful cloth that is handwoven and worn in much of Africa.

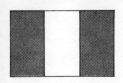

AKWA NWA NERE NNWA
(The Little Nanny)
Nigeria

Call: **Och' iyi che nkolu yi:**

Response: **Iwele**

(continue throughout) **Och' iyi che nkolu yi:**

Iwele

Oku mmili nabo mu nalu nnwa

Iwele

Asimu chube Ngene Eze-Oba

Iwele

Asimu chube Ngene Iyineli

Iwele

Iyi negbu amuma k' oda negbu

Iwele

Mmili sol' ogugu naa nenu

Iwele

Olie mu,

Iwele

Oraa mu, k' odil' Eze-Oba

Iwele.

This is the story of a little nanny who is sent to the river to fetch more water for the baby. It is a dangerous task because mean spirits and the king of the alligators live there.

She sings this song to the guardian spirit and tells him her trouble. According to the story the spirit takes pity on her and actually fetches the water for her. She returns home happy and smiling.

Nigeria has more people than any other African country. Many of them live in large modern cities but most Nigerians live in rural areas and follow the traditions of their ancestors. Their stories have often been passed by word of mouth for generations rather than written down. This song is in the Ibo language.

BEBE MOKE
(Baby So Small)

Zaire

Be- be mo -ke,   na - ni a- be - ti yo,
Ba- by so small, hush now,— don't you cry,

Lo- ba na   nga, Ngai pe na- zon- gi- sa.
Tell me what's wrong, I'll take— care of you.

Mba- la mo- su - su o- tu - ta - ni na
You are—— safe now,— close your eyes,—

mur ya nda— ko.
Hush-a, hush-a- bye.

In Zaire, the Congo River flows through one of the largest jungles in the world. Many interesting wild animals live in Zaire including zebras, antelope, rhinoceroses, gorillas, elephants, giraffes, leopards, lions, and monkeys. This song is sung in Lingala, one of 200 languages spoken in Zaire. Lingala is the language of music. Often older children care for their younger brothers and sisters and they sing this song while rocking the little ones in their arms.

KANYONI KANJA
(Little Bird Outside)

Kenya

Ka-nyo-ni ka-nja, ka-nyo-ni ka-
Lit-tle bird out-side, lit-tle bird out-

nja Ga-ku-gwa-nja na mĩ-the-ko.
side Gai-ly laugh-ing and rol-ling 'round.

2. Ndakoria atĩrĩ, ndakoria atĩrĩ,
   "Wamĩcore watinda ku?"

3. "Ndatinda kairi, ndatinda kairi
   Ngiaragania mbĩrĩgĩtĩ."

4. "Ĩ mbĩrĩgĩtĩ, ĩ mbĩrĩgĩtĩ
   Na ndinainũ kia kagoto."

5. "Kagũa irianĩ? Kagũa irianĩ?"
   "Gwa cũ cũ wa kamirũkio."

2. When I ask of it, when I ask of it,
   "Little striped one, where have you been?"

3. "At the quarry* near, at the quarry near
   Spreading big rocks and little stones.

4. "All the rocks I left, all the rocks I left
   And I lost all my little stones."

5. "Where, you lost them where? Where, you lost them where?"
   "All the stones fell into the sea."

* a place where stone is excavated (dug out)

This song is sung in Kikuyu, although the national language of Kenya is Swahili. Many tourists go on safaris (expeditions) in Kenya on game preserves (protected areas) to see wild animals such as elephants, giraffes, lions, rhinoceroses, and zebras.

49

Asia

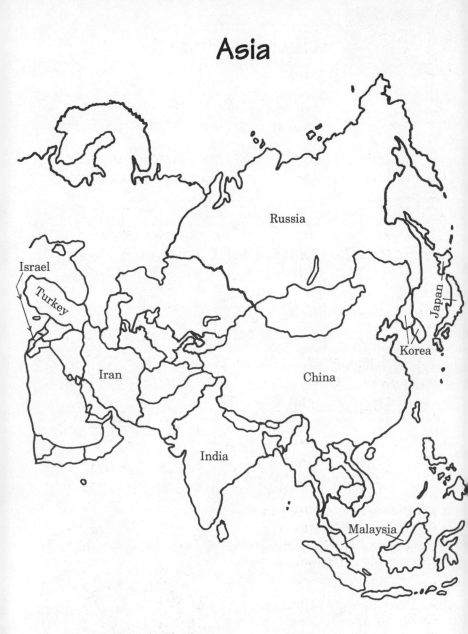

ALİ BABA'NIN ÇİFTLİĞİ
(Ali Baba's Farm)

Turkey

1. Al- i Ba-ba-'nın bir çift-li-ği var,
Al- i Ba-ba, he has a lit-tle farm,

Çift- li - ğin- de ku - zu - la - rı var,
On his farm he has some lit- tle lambs,

"Mee, Mee," di - ye ba - ğı - rır
"Baa, Baa," cry his lit- tle lambs,

Çift- li - ğin- de Al - i Ba-ba-'nın.
On the farm of Al - i Ba - ba.

2. Ali Baba'nın bir çiftliği var,
Çiftliğinde inekleri var,
"Möö, möö," diye bağırır,
Çiftliğinde Ali Baba'nın.

3. ...horozları... "ü ü rü, ü ü rü"...

2. Ali Baba, he has a little farm,
On his farm he has some little cows,
"Moo, moo," cry his little cows,
On the farm of Ali Baba.

3. ...roosters... "oo oo roo, oo oo roo"...

Turkey lies both in Europe and Asia and has been a bridge between the two continents for centuries. The highest mountain in Turkey is Mt. Ararat which some people believe is where Noah's ark landed after the flood. Over half the workers of Turkey are farmers.

ZUM GALI GALI

Israel

Em Chant (throughout song) | **Fine**

Zum ga-li, ga-li, ga-li, zum ga-li, ga-li, zum!

Verse

1. He-cha-lutz le maan a-vo-da,
Pi-o-neers all work as____ one,

D.C. al Fine

A-vo-da le maan he-cha-lutz.
Work as one all pi-o-neers.

2. **Ha shalom le maan ha amin,
Ha amin le maan ha shalom.**

2. Peace shall be for all the world,
All the world shall be for peace.

Suggestion: Fade out with chant until end. On final "Zum," shout it out and extend arm over head.

זוּם גָּלִי גָּלִי גָּלִי
זוּם גָּלִי גָּלִי
הֶחָלוּץ לְמַעַן עֲבוֹדָה
עֲבוֹדָה לְמַעַן הֶחָלוּץ

הַשָּׁלוֹם לְמַעַן הָעַמִּים
הָעַמִּים לְמַעַן הַשָּׁלוֹם

Lyrics in Hebrew

The people of Israel are hard workers who have turned a barren, unproductive land into a very prosperous country. Ancient Israel was the traditional homeland of the Jewish people. It is also the birthplace of Christianity.

52

ATTAL, MATTAL

Iran

Attal, Mattal, tu tu le,
Ghave Hassan che ju re?
Na shir da re, na pestoon.
Ghave sho borde hendestoon
Yek zane hendi bessoon.
Esme sho bezar Amgazee
Ture tomoonesh ghermezi
Hacheeno wacheen,
Ye pato varcheen.

Attal, Mattal, hey, hey hey!
How is Hassan's cow today?
"She has no more milk," he said,
So to India she was led;
Traded for a girl to wed.
Pretty girl named Amgazee,
Skirts with red lace to her knee.
To her knee? To her knee!

اَتَل مَتَل توتوله   کاوِ حُسَن چه جوره
نه شیر داره نه پستون   کاوشُ بُرده هِندستون
یك زن هندی پستون
اِسمشو بِذار عَم قزی   دور دامنش قرمزی
ها چینُ و واچین
یك پا تُ وَر چین

Lyrics in Persian

Formation: Children sit on floor in circle with knees drawn up, feet together. Leader is in center of circle.

Actions: Leader goes around circle patting knees one at a time in rhythm with chant. Knee touched on last syllable of chant is removed. (Keeping leg bent, lower knee sideways to floor) Chant is repeated over and over, one knee being eliminated each time until only one remains. That person is the winner and becomes the new leader. Game begins again.

Iran, originally part of ancient Persia, is one of the world's oldest countries, its history dating back almost 5,000 years. Most Iranians are Muslims and the Islamic faith strongly influences government and the way of life. Iran is famous for its Persian rugs which are beautiful, detailed handwoven rugs.

ANILAE, ANILAE
(Chipmunk, Chipmunk)

India

An - i - lae, an - i - lae, va, va,
Chip - munk, chip - munk, come, come,

va, Ay - a - gi - ya an - i - lae,
come, Beau - ti - ful chip - munk,

Fine

va, va, va. Goi - ya ma - ram
come, come, come. Climb way up the

D.C. al Fine

ye - re - va, Gun - du pa - yam kon - du - va.
gua - va tree, Bring a ripe fruit back to me.

அணிலே அணிலே வா வா வா
அழகிய அணிலே வா வா வா
கொய்யா மரம் ஏறி வா
குண்டு பழம் கொண்டு வா

Lyrics in Tamil

KAI VEECHAMMA
(Move Your Hand)

[a]Kai veechamma, [a]kai veesu,
[b]Kadaiku pohalam, [a]kai veesu,
[c]Meetai vangalam, [a]kai veesu,
[d]Meduvai thingalam, [a]kai veesu.

[a]Move your hand, [a]move your hand,
[b]Let's go to the store, [a]move your hand,
[c]Let's buy candy now, [a]move your hand,
[d]Let's eat slowly now, [a]move your hand.

Actions:
a) Elbow at side, hand out in front, move forearm back and forth.
b) Put fingertips together to form a roof.
c) With thumb and two fingers, pretend to hold candy, twist back and forth.
d) Put hand to mouth, pretend to eat candy.

India has a very large population. Although there are modern cities, most people live in small villages which consist of mud and straw huts crowded together. Cows are considered sacred in the Hindu religion and often roam freely, even in cities. Hindi is India's national language but this song and poem are in Tamil, one of the 14 major languages.

54

FONG SWEI
(After School)

China

Gung ke — wan bi — ti yang syi.
School is — out and the sun is low.

Shou shr — shu bao hwei jya — chu.
I take my books and home I go.

Jyan liao — fu mu — xing ge li.
My par-ents wait so — pa - tient-ly.

Fu mu — dwei wo — shiao syi syi.
I bow to them and they smile at me.

功	課	完	畢	太	陽	西
拿	起	書	包	回	家	去
看	見	父	母	行	個	禮
父	母	對	我	笑	嘻	嘻

Lyrics in Chinese

China is the third largest country in the world and has the largest population. This song is in Mandarin, the official language of China. Early Chinese music sounds different from Western music because it uses a five-tone scale instead of eight. To hear this scale, use the black keys on the piano.

ARIRANG

Korea

A - ri-rang,— a - ri-rang,— a-ra - ri -
A - ri-rang,— a - ri-rang,— a-ra - ri -

yo,——— A - ri-rang— ko - gae - rŭl—
yo,——— O - ver the— A - ri - rang—

no - mo - gan - da. Na - rŭl pŏ - ri - go
Hill you must go. How I wish you would

ka - shi - nŭn - nim— ŭn,——— Shim - ni - do—
not go— a - way,——— It is such a

mot— ka— so— bal - byong - nan - da.
long— walk— and I want you to stay.

*This is the flag of South Korea

Lyrics in Korean

아리랑 아리랑 아라리요.
아리랑 고개를 넘어간다.
나를 버리고 가시는 님은.
십리도 못가서 발병 난다.

The two nations of North Korea and South Korea are a peninsula. Off the southern coast of Korea is Chae Chu Island where Hae Nyo (Ocean Girls) dive for pearls. The girls begin diving at age seven and dive up to sixty feet without any breathing equipment.

56

AME, AME
(Rain Song)

Japan

1. A - me, a - me, fur - e, fur - e, ka-a-
Rain-ing, rain-ing, how it's rain - ing, rain a

san - ga, Jya-no me de o mu kae,—
lit-tle more, Moth-er's bring-ing my um-brel-la,

u - re shi - na. Pi chi, pi chi,
it can rain and pour. Pit-ter, pat-ter,

cha pu, cha pu, ran, ran, ran.
pit - ter, pat - ter, drip, drip, drop.

あめ
あめ
ふれ
ふれ
かあさんが
じゃのめで
おむかえ
うれしいな
ぴちぴち
ちゃぷちゃぷ
らんらんらん

Lyrics in Japanese

Japan, sometimes called the "Land of the Rising Sun," is a chain of volcanic islands. Japanese is one of the several languages written by using "characters" which are small line drawings that represent entire words or ideas. They are read from top to bottom, right to left.

57

POK AMAI, AMAI
(Clap Together)

Malaysia

1. Pok a - mai, a - mai,   Be - la - lang ku -
Clap, clap, clap your hands,   Dra - gon - fly and

pu ku - pu,   Ber - te - pok a - dik pan -
but - ter - fly,   You can do it, yes you

dai   Ma - lam u - pah su - su.
can,   Then you'll have milk to - night.

2. Susu lemak manis,
   Santan kelapa muda,
   Adik jangan menangis,
   Emak nak buat kerja.

2. The milk is sweet and mild,
   From the coconut it comes,
   Don't cry now little child,
   Til mother's work is done.

Malaysia is almost entirely mountains and mostly covered with tropical rain forests. The climate is always hot and wet. Leafy rubber trees in Malaysia produce more rubber than any other country.

Australia & Oceania

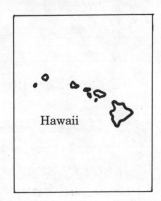

Hawaii

Australia

New Zealand

KOOKABURRA

(Round)

Australia

1. Koo-ka-bur-ra sits in the old gum tree,—

Mer - ry, mer - ry king of the bush is he,—

Laugh, Koo-ka-bur-ra, laugh, Koo-ka-bur-ra,

Gay your life must be.

2. Kookaburra sits in the old gum tree,
   Eating all the gumdrops he can see,
   Stop, Kookaburra, stop, Kookaburra,
   Leave some there for me.

Australia is the only country that is also a continent. Many unusual animals live there including kangaroos, koalas, platypuses and wombats. The kookaburra is a bird found only in Australia. Its call sounds like laughter.

EPO I TAI TAI E
(I Will Be Happy)

New Zealand
Maori

E - po i tai tai e, e - po i tai tai e,

E - po i tai tai, e - po i tu - ki - tu - ki,

E - po i tu - ki - tu - ki e.

Meaning: I will not be sad, I will be happy.

New Zealand consists of two main islands and dozens of smaller islands. It is a beautiful country of snow-capped mountains, green lowlands, beaches, lakes, and waterfalls. Kiwi is a nickname for a New Zealander. It is also the name of a fruit and a New Zealand bird that cannot fly. This is a folk song of the Maoris, the first inhabitants of New Zealand, who belong to the Polynesian race.

NANI WALE NA HALA
(Pretty Hala Trees)

Hawaii

Na-ni wa-le na— ha-la, E-a, e-a.
Pret-ty are the ha-la trees,— E-a, e-a.

O Na-u-e i-ke ka-i, E-a, e-a.
Sway-ing in the warm sea breeze,— E-a, e-a.

Ke— on-i a— e-la, E-a, e-a.
Cling-ing to the sands be-low,— E-a, e-a.

Pi-li ma-i Ha—e-na, E-a, e-a.
Near Ha-e-na where they grow,— E-a, e-a.

Formation:
Kneel and sit on heels with a puili stick* in each hand.

Actions:
a) Cross sticks and tap once out in front
b) Uncross sticks and tap once on floor
c) Cross sticks and tap once overhead
d) Tap right shoulder with right stick
e) Tap left shoulder with left stick
f) Cross sticks and tap four times overhead from left to right (making an arc in the air)
g) Cross sticks and tap four times overhead from right to left

*A puili stick is a piece of bamboo with long slits at one end, leaving a handle on the other.

Hawaii, the 50th state of the U.S., is made up of islands near the middle of the Pacific Ocean. The original settlers were Polynesians. Hawaii is well–known for the hula (dance), leis (flower wreaths), luaus (feasts), and the greeting "aloha." From Hala trees, Hawaiians make baskets, hats, sleeping mats, and paint brushes.

INDEX

Africa Map 45
Akwa Nwa Nere Nnwa (The Little Nanny) *Nigeria* 47
Alle Eendjes (All The Ducklings) *The Netherlands* 34
Alle Meine Entlein (All My Little Ducklings) *Germany* 38
Ali Babanin Çiftligi (Ali Baba's Farm) *Turkey* 51
Ame, Ame (Rain Song) *Japan* 57
Anilae, Anilae (Chipmunk, Chipmunk) *India* 54
Arirang *Korea* 56
Asia Map 50
Attal, Mattal *Iran* 53
Australia & Oceania Map..59
Bebe Moke (Baby So Small) *Zaire* 48
Brown Girl In The Ring *Guyana* 19
Chi Chi Bud (Chi Chi Bird) *Jamaica* 17
Ciranda (Circle Game) *Brazil*..20
Coulter's Candy *Scotland* 32
Eentsy Weentsy Spider *United States* 13
El Coquí (The Frog) *Puerto Rico*..16
En Enebær Busk (The Mulberry Bush) *Denmark* 28
Epo I Tai Tai E (I Will Be Happy) *New Zealand*......................61
Europe Map...25
Fong Swei (After School) *China* 55
Frère Jacques (Brother John) *France* 35
Going Over The Sea *Canada* 10
Hello To All The Children Of The World 6
Kai Veechamma (Move Your Hand) *India* 54
Kanyoni Kanja (Little Bird Outside) *Kenya* 49
Kookaburra *Australia*..60
Lavender's Blue *England* 33
Los Pollitos (The Little Chicks) *Peru* 24
Mi Burro (My Burro) *Spain*..40
Mi Chacra (My Farm) *Argentina*..22
Mio Galletto (My Little Rooster) *Italy*..................................39
Nani Wale Na Hala (Pretty Hala Trees) *Hawaii*......................62
North America Map...9
Piiri Pieni Pyörii (The Circle Goes Around) *Finland* 30
Pin Pón *Mexico*..14
Pok Amai, Amai (Clap Together) *Malaysia* 58
Pou 'n–do To Dachtilidi (Where Is The Ring) *Greece*................42
Ringe, Ringe Raja (Ring Around Raja) *Yugoslavia* 43
Ro, Ro Til Fiskeskjær (Row, Row To The Fishing Spot) *Norway* ..26

Små Grodorna (Little Frogs) *Sweden* 27
South America Map...18
Tingalayo *West Indies*..15
Tue Tue *Ghana* 46
Uhe´ Basho^n Sho^n (The Crooked Path) *United States* 12
Vesyoliye Gusi (Jolly, Happy Ganders) *Ukraine* 44
Wee Falorie Man *Ireland*..31
Weggis Zue (Swiss Hiking Song) *Switzerland*............................36
World Map 8
Zum Gali Gali *Israel* 52

Thanks also to our musicians:
Canada, United States & English translations—Wee Singers; **United States (Omaha Indian)**—*Iron Eye Singers* (Cameron Smith, Francis Merrick, Landis Merrick, RedWing Stabler) ; **Mexico, Argentina, Peru**—Verónica Thomann, María José Toledo, María Paula Toledo, *Grupo Condor* (José M. Toledo, Gerardo Calderon G., Rogelio Rangel T., Otto Gygax); **Brazil**—Isamira Boyington, *Grupo Condor*; **West Indies, Jamaica**—Alexander Duncan, Brian Healey, Denise Valient Healey; **Guyana**—Alexander Duncan; **Puerto Rico**—Osbaldo Ocasio, David Larsen, John Hughes, Luis Opazo; **Norway**—Lilla Larsen; **Sweden**—Tami Gebhardt; **Denmark**—Karin Taidal ; **Finland**—Portland Finnish School (Kai Ojala, Mia Ojala, Daniel Brooks, Mari Nelson, Tiina Nelson, Suvi Chisholm, Mairi Chisholm, Hanna Brooks); **Ireland & Scotland**—*Erin Aire* (Doug Hamar, Vicki Clark, Charlie Hyman, Judith Bows, Gail Gibbard); **England**—Sue Sumpter; **The Netherlands**—Tineke Bierma; **France**—Portland French–American School (Caetlin Folawn, Anna Campbell, Laurel Nugent, Elizabeth Campbell, Anna Kern, Joseph Gardner); **Switzerland**—Shirley Abbott Clark; **Germany**—Sylvia Groener; **Italy**—Elisa Allegri De Leonardis; **Spain**—Rafaela de Cádiz, José Solano; **Greece**—Greek School of the Holy Trinity Greek Orthodox Church, Pete Helfand, Michael Beach; **Yugoslavia**—Joan Gaustad, Roy Torley; **Ukraine**—Ilya Katsel, Marianna Yablonsky, Jania Yablonsky, Roy Torley; **Ghana**—Kwaku Mensah, Mai Chi Maraire; **Nigeria**—Nnamdi Emetarom, Suzanne Emetarom; **Zaire**—Antonio Gaspar; **Kenya**—Mary Mutitu, Mai Chi Maraire; **Turkey**—Şermin Emre Özgür, Michael Beach, Pete Helfand, J. Michael Kearsey; **Israel**—Portland Jewish Academy (Louis Olenick, Leila Raphael, Sheerya Shivers, Rachel Stampfer, Eli Kwitman, David Berdichevsky, Harry Frishberg); **Iran**—Kianoosh Shokohian, Michael Beach; **India**—Arundati Gopinath, Vaijayanthi Gopinath, Rik Masterson; **China**—Cheng Yanping; **Korea**—Kathy Jin Hagen; **Japan**—Maiko Shiota, Kanako Shiota; **Malaysia**—I'Kaika Seth Young, Kakani Katija Young; **Australia**—Bryant Easterman; **New Zealand**—Richard Belog, Kavesi Matau; **Hawaii**—Richard Belog, Ryan Smythe, Sam Kama; ...And to Barry Hagen, Mauri Macy, Dan Portis–Cathers, Gary Hobbs, and Hilary Beall.